Leah Komaiko

I LIKE THE MUSIC

pictures by Barbara Westman

FLASH

HarperTrophy®
A Division of HarperCollins*Publishers*

I Like the Music
Text copyright © 1987 by Leah Komaiko
Illustrations copyright © 1987 by Barbara Westman
Printed in the U.S.A. All rights reserved.
Library of Congress Cataloging-in-Publication Data
Komaiko, Leah
  I like the music.

  Summary: A little girl who loves street music learns
to love the symphony as well when her grandmother
takes her to an outdoor concert.
  [1. Music—Fiction.   2. Stories in rhyme]
I. Westman, Barbara, ill.   II. Title.
PZ8.K835Ia1   1987   [E]   87-170
ISBN 0-06-023271-4
ISBN 0-06-023272-2 (lib. bdg.)
ISBN 0-06-443189-4 (pbk.)
First Harper Trophy edition, 1989.
❖
Visit us on the World Wide Web!
http://www.harperchildrens.com

For my family, who is the music
L.K.

For Arthur
B.W.

I do not like this concert hall.
This concert hall's no fun at all.
The orchestra just plays and plays,
I could be here for thirty days.
And I must sit here in this seat,
Don't clap your hands,
Don't tap your feet,
And Grandma says this is a treat.

But I like the music in the street. . . .

I like the music
When the junkman finds a blues stick
And shabops-it
On the tops-it
Of the garbage cans.
And his wife plays the fiddle
And their monkey in the middle
From the Congos
Plays the bongos
On the pots and pans.

I like the beat
Of my feet
When my shoes hit the street
And I rapa-tapa-tapa
On the hot concrete.
No parade,
Just the maid
With her Dixieland mop,
Soppin' with the boppin'
All around the bus stop.

But Grandma says the symphony,
The symphony's the place to be.

She thinks that this is one big treat,
But I like the music in the street.

When they sing...
Come on over—
Ain't you heard?
Papa's goin' out to buy
A lullaby bird.
It plays the pianie,
It sings on top of Grannie,
And all it eats for supper
Is a rotten old bananie.
So don't sleep, baby,
Dance instead.
The bees are on the ceiling,
The donkey's in the shed.
You play your ukelele,
I got my saxophones,
So Tom Cat, play the tom-toms,
And Bulldog, play those bones.

But Grandma says the symphony,
The symphony's the thing for me,
So we'll hear one on Saturday.
I will not go.
I'll run away!
Then Grandma says,
"You've never tried
A concert that is played outside.
This orchestra plays in the park
And doesn't start till after dark."

The dark?
The park?

Why Grandma, this treat sounds just right.
I like the music late at night....

I like the tuning
When the man is in the mooning
And he plays the big bassooning
In the key of C.
And the strings bow and pick it
To the clicks of the cricket,
And coyotes
Sing their noteys
For the timpani.

Now the tuba's here from Cuba,
The French horn's here from France,
And I came all the way from home
To cha-cha with the saxophone,
But he's gone to a dance.
So people from the palace
And people from the streets
Kindly rapa-tapa-tapa
All around your seats.

And now it's dark as dark can be
And this is the best I know—
When the firefly
Lights the night sky
So the moths can see the show.
And the spotlight
Makes the stage bright,
It is all about to start.
I can feel the flutes are fluttering
All around my beating heart.

And the airplanes wink down at me,
There's no waiting anymore—
Drums! Here comes Mr. Conductor
From behind his small trapdoor.
He walks and walks across the stage,
He takes a little bow,
He turns to greet the audience
And orchestra, and now...

He lifts his eyes
In great surprise,
Here are his first commands—
"I can't conduct all this alone,
I've only got two hands!
I must have one assistant,
But just who will that one be?"
Lucky night—
I like the music
When the conductor is me!
Now everyone applauds me
As I walk down through the crowd.
And the bass hands me the baton
And my grandma is so proud
As I curtsey to the maestro
And salute the violin,

Rapa-tap my new one-two stick,
And now, Everyone...
BEGIN!